Bella's Birthday Bounce

Written by Jill Atkins

Illustrated by

Eleftheria-Garyfallia Leftheri

WAYLAND

Bella's Birthday Bounce

First published in 2009
by Wayland

Text copyright © Jill Atkins
Illustration copyright © Eleftheria-Garyfallia Leftheri

Wayland
338 Euston Road
London NW1 3BH

Wayland Australia
Hachette Children's Books
Level 17/207 Kent Street
Sydney, NSW 2000

Series Editor: Louise John
Editor: Katie Powell
Cover design: Paul Cherrill
Design: D.R.ink
Consultant: Shirley Bickler

A CIP catalogue record for this book is available from the British Library.

ISBN 9780750258005

Printed in China

Wayland is a division of Hachette Children's Books,
an Hachette UK company
www.hachette.co.uk

Bella loved to bounce.
Boing! She bounced on her bed.

Boing! She bounced downstairs.

Boing! She bounced into
the kitchen.

She knocked over the milk jug.
"Oh, Bella!" said Mum.

"What are we going to do
with you?" said Dad.

The next day was Bella's birthday.
Mad Uncle Albert came to tea.
"I know you like bouncing," he said,
"so I made you these."

He gave her two giant springs fixed to a pair of wooden shoes.

"Try them on," he said.

Bella fixed them to her feet.
Then she stood up.

"Wow!" she said. "Hey, everyone,
look what Uncle Albert made me!"

"They look great!" said Charlie.
"Come on, Bella," said Uncle Albert.
"Let's try them out."

Boing! Boing! Boing!
Bella was off down the street.
Uncle Albert ran beside her.

Mum, Dad and Charlie tried
to keep up.

"This is fun," Bella shouted.

Boing! Boing! Bella bounced over garden fences.

She bounced over parked cars.

She knocked over dustbins and she frightened cats.

"Thanks, Uncle Albert," she shouted. "This is the best present I've ever had."

Soon they reached the end
of the street.
"Time to stop!" panted
 Uncle Albert.

"I can't!" Bella shouted.

She bounced towards the farm.
Soon, Uncle Albert and the others
were far behind.

Suddenly, a tractor drove out in front of her. Bella put her hands over her eyes.

19

Swish! The springs hit the top of the straw. Crash! The straw fell down.

She bounced into a field, and she frightened all the sheep away.

Bella was heading for the duck pond.
"Help!" she yelled. "Stop me!"

Splash! She landed in the pond.

Quack! The ducks flew away.

Uncle Albert pulled Bella out of the pond as the farmer ran towards them.

"Oh, no!" Bella said. "He's going to be so cross."

"Don't worry," said Mad Uncle Albert. "I've got an idea."

Uncle Albert ran to meet the farmer. They chatted, then they shook hands.

"I'll make some more pairs of springs," said Uncle Albert.
"What for?" asked Bella.
"Wait and see," said Uncle Albert.

And, the next day, the whole family had the best time...

...picking apples for the farmer!

START READING is a series of highly enjoyable books for beginner readers. **The books have been carefully graded to match the Book Bands widely used in schools.** This enables readers to be sure they choose books that match their own reading ability.

Look out for the Band colour on the book in our Start Reading logo.

The Bands are:

- Pink Band 1
- Red Band 2
- Yellow Band 3
- Blue Band 4
- Green Band 5
- Orange Band 6
- Turquoise Band 7
- Purple Band 8
- Gold Band 9

START READING books can be read independently or shared with an adult. They promote the enjoyment of reading through satisfying stories supported by fun illustrations.

Jill Atkins used to be a teacher, but she now spends her time writing for children. She is married with two grown-up children, three grandsons and a granddaughter. She loves cats and wishes she had had an uncle like Albert when she was a little girl!

Eleftheria-Garyfallia Leftheri was given a flying train for her seventh birthday. She travelled into magical worlds, where she met many mystical creatures. When she grew up, she decided to study languages so that she could talk to them, illustration so she could draw them and animation so she could make them move.